Animals should definitely <u>not</u> wear clothing.

Written by Judi Barrett

illustrated by Ron Barrett

Aladdin Paperbacks

New York   London   Toronto   Sydney

For Amy and Valerie

ALADDIN PAPERBACKS
An imprint of Simon & Schuster Children's Publishing Division
1230 Avenue of the Americas, New York, NY 10020
Text copyright © 1970 by Judi Barrett
Copyright renewed © 1998 by Judi Barrett
Illustrations copyright © 1970 by Ron Barrett
Copyright renewed © 1998 by Ron Barrett
ALADDIN PAPERBACKS and colophon are trademarks of Simon & Schuster, Inc.
Manufactured in China
First Aladdin Paperbacks edition 1974
Second Aladdin Paperbacks edition 1989
This Aladdin Paperbacks edition January 2006
10 9 8 7 6 5 4 3 2
The Library of Congress has cataloged the second Aladdin Paperbacks edition as follows:
Barrett, Judi.
Animals should definitely *not* wear clothing.
Summary: Pictures of animals wearing clothes show why this would be a ridiculous custom for
them to adopt.
ISBN-13: 978-0-689-20592-7 (hc.)
ISBN-10: 0-689-20592-9 (hc.)
1. Animals—Juvenile humor. 2. American wit and humor, Pictorial. 3. Animals—Caricatures and
cartoons. [1. Animals—Wit and humor] I. Barrett, Ron, ill. II. Title.
[PN6231.A5B364 1988] 818'.5402 88-7825
ISBN-13: 978-1-4169-1232-3 (Aladdin pbk.)
ISBN-10: 1-4169-1232-0 (Aladdin pbk.)
1017 SCP

Animals should definitely not wear clothing...

because
it would be
disastrous for
a porcupine,

because
a camel
might wear it
in the wrong
places,

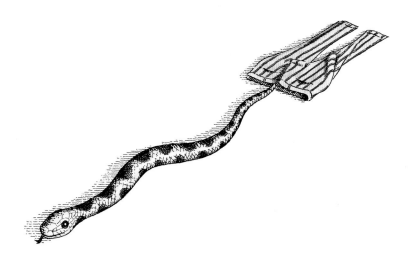

because
a snake would
lose it,

because
a mouse
could get lost
in it,

because
a sheep
might find it
terribly hot,

because
it could be
very messy
for a pig,

because
it might
make life hard
for a hen,

**because
a kangaroo
would find it
quite
unnecessary,**

because
a giraffe
might look
sort of silly,

because
a billy goat
would eat it
for lunch,

because
it would always
be wet
on a walrus,

**because
a moose
could never
manage,**

because opossums might wear it upside down by mistake,

and most of all, because it might be very embarrassing.

Judi Barrett divides her days between teaching art to children and writing children's books.

Ron Barrett spends his nights illustrating the books she writes, and his days as an Art Director at a New York advertising agency.

Animals should definitely not wear clothing is their second book. Their first one was *Old MacDonald Had An Apartment House.*

They both firmly believe that animals should definitely not wear clothing, except for an occasional dog coat on below freezing days.

This is where they draw the line.